Once Upon a Twist

Rosabella and the Three Bears

Once Upon a
Twist

Rosabella and the
Three Bears

Perdita Finn

LITTLE, BROWN AND COMPANY
New York Boston

Cover design by Ching Chan and Véronique L. Sweet.
Cover illustration by Erwin Madrid.

Little, Brown and Company
Hachette Book Group
1290 Avenue of the Americas, New York, NY 10104
Visit us at lb-kids.com
everafterhigh.com

First Edition: July 2017

Little, Brown and Company is a division of Hachette Book Group, Inc. The Little, Brown name and logo are trademarks of Hachette Book Group, Inc.

The publisher is not responsible for websites (or their content) that are not owned by the publisher.

Library of Congress Control Number 2017933408

ISBNs: 978-0-316-46496-3 (pbk.), 978-0-316-46495-6 (ebook)

Printed in the United States of America

LSC-C

10 9 8 7 6 5 4 3 2 1

For Kadence Jade,

princess in training!

CHAPTER 1

The Case of the Mixed-Up Cheerhex

Faybelle frowned. Her cheerhex wasn't working as well as she had planned! It was supposed to put the wrong characters into the wrong stories for their hexams. It was supposed to cause all kinds of mischief and mayhem. But these princesses kept Happily-Ever-Aftering their endings!

Briar Beauty was twirling her hair around her finger and chatting with Apple White.

"Can you believe Cupid landed in Ashlynn's story at a ball with a missing sneaker? But I heard that it ended pretty Happily Ever After," she said with a smile.

"That's even more upside-down and backward than Wonderland," agreed Apple White.

Faybelle loudly sighed, disappointed, as she eavesdropped. These mix-ups were supposed to cause a lot more chaos and confusion.

Across the room, Cupid was smiling brightly as she told a bunch of classmates about how much she'd enjoyed meeting the wicked stepsisters. "They're not bad at all when you get to know them," she was saying.

Faybelle rolled her eyes. She opened up her notebook and started making a list of *Dark Fairy Dos* and *Dark Fairy Don'ts*:

- *Dark Fairies* do *cast spells that cause lots of trouble.*
- *Dark Fairies* don't *let things work out happily and well!*

Hmmmm, Faybelle considered. She couldn't wait for the next fairytale mix-up. She needed something to darken her day.

Who would it be next? Maybe this time nothing would go right!

"I wonder…" Faybelle said out loud.

Briar caught sight of Faybelle's beaming face, which seemed to worry her. "Faybelle, are you up to something?"

Faybelle wanted to tell someone about her cheerhex, but she knew in order for her hex to keep working, she had to keep it a secret.

Faybelle was going to make sure the stories *stayed* scrambled.

"Nothing, Briar. Today's lunch just smells wicked-good."

Briar nodded in agreement and Faybelle sighed with relief. Her secret was safe.

Faybelle smiled to herself. She rubbed her hands together, hoping that her hex would start to *really* cause mayhem in these storybooks. Maybe she would finally have something really vile to brag about in Villain Club!

Chapter 2

Not a Clue!

Crrrack! Rosabella Beauty crashed through the trees and landed on big, soft spot of green moss. She brushed some leaves off her yellow dress and pulled a twig out of her long brown-and-red hair. All around her were blurry red spots and tiny, dark shapes. Her glasses must have fallen off when she dropped into the storybook for her midterm hexam!

But something did not feel just right to Rosabella. What had just happened? Where was she? Tall trees rose above her. There were birds singing. She was supposed to be in her fairytale for her midterm hexam, but this didn't seem right to her. She must be in a forest, but it didn't look like the Enchanted Forest near Ever After High. Could it be the dreaded Dark Forest? She shuddered. She couldn't tell. Everything was so blurry. Everything was so fuzzy. Where could she possibly be?

Rosabella realized that she must've landed in the wrong storybook. Was this a surprise portion of her midterm hexam? Suddenly, Rosabella was nervous. She hadn't studied for surprises!

"Oh my!" chirped a small voice. "Are these your glasses?"

Rosabella squinted. She couldn't find whoever was speaking…but something sparkling caught her eye. Her glasses! She slipped them back on. *That's much better!*

She looked around her. The red blurs were flowers, and the dark shapes were little birds. But even though she could see the trees more clearly now, she still didn't recognize this forest. They didn't look like the kinds of trees in the forest that surrounded her castle. How strange!

"I don't think I've seen you around here before," squeaked the voice again. Rosabella looked down by her feet and saw a little bucktoothed squirrel speaking right to her!

"You can speak? This can't be my forest…" Rosabella said thoughtfully. She knew there weren't any speaking animals in her story.

The squirrel's nose wiggled up and down. His tail twitched. He seemed confused.

"I'm Rosabella," she hexplained. "I hope I didn't frighten you before. Do you know the way to the Beast's castle?"

"The Beast?!" squealed the squirrel, alarmed.

"Oh no! A beast! A beast!" someone cried. A little salamander who was scrambling by had overheard them.

A crow squawked loudly. "A beast! A beast! A beast!"

It seemed that Rosabella had said something wrong, and she didn't like to see any animal upset—especially not by her!

"Are *you* the Beast?" The squirrel rubbed his paws together nervously.

"No!" Rosabella laughed. "I'm the *daughter* of Beauty and the Beast, though I think I'm in the wrong storybook." Rosabella paused to consider how nervous all the animals were acting. No matter which storybook she'd landed in, Rosabella couldn't just leave these poor creatures when they were so worried! "But my story isn't important right now. It looks like something's upsetting all of you. Can I help?"

The birds gathered around, tweeting and flapping their wings. The salamander began making hissing noises. The squirrel was chattering a mile a minute.

"Our nests were just a jumble of sticks!"

"A beast overturned our rocks!"

"Are you the one blowing down our houses?" The squirrel was looking up at her, his little black eyes worried.

"Oh no!" Rosabella replied reassuringly. She was sad to see the woodland creatures so worried, and she wanted to make them smile. Then she had an idea!

"Watch—I can hardly blow a leaf past the tip of my nose!" She picked up an oak leaf and tried to blow it. It stuck to the end of her nose. The sight made the squirrel giggle. He thumped his tail as he saw she was telling the truth. The salamander grinned.

But Rosabella still didn't know where she was. She wondered if Daring Charming had also landed in this strange fairytale, since he was the Beast to her Beauty. "Has anyone seen a prince around?" she asked.

But no one had.

I wish I could take a quick trip to the Legacy Orchard right about now and do some research on strange forests and talking animals! This is definitely someone else's story, she thought.

Still, it sounded like this forest had a mystery that needed solving and some animals that needed helping. Rosabella was always looking out for woodland friends in trouble.

"Watch out!" It was a little butterfly with spotted wings, staring up at her. Her boot was just about to land on him.

"Whoops! I'm sorry," Rosabella said, jumping carefully out of the way. She was going to have to be fairy careful, she realized.

Rosabella didn't want to cause any trouble in this mysterious fairytale. She didn't want to take this story off book! So she made sure to walk between the bushes and the flowers, and she smiled at all the butterflies. When she knocked a stick or a fallen leaf out of place, she put it right back where it belonged. Still, she noticed the deer scampered away from her and the owls swooped through the trees as she passed.

"Who! Who! *Whodunnit?*" they hooted.

Rosabella was fairy sensitive, and she could tell that all the creatures she met were nervous and frightened. What were they all so scared of? Should she be scared, too?

She peered into the shadows, but she didn't see anything scary—and she didn't *feel* anything scary, either…and she usually did if there was trouble afoot.

Jumping into someone else's storybook was a lot of work. Soon Rosabella started to feel really tired. And hungry! Her stomach rumbled, and she wondered if she could persuade any of the squirrels to help her find some nuts.

A beam of golden light was shining through the trees. At first, Rosabella thought it must be the early-morning sunshine, but as she got closer, she saw it was coming from a window in a cottage. Smoke was rising up out of the chimney, and a delicious smell was wafting from the open door.

"Looks like someone might be home," she noted to herself. "And something sugary and sweet is on the stove!"

Rosabella made her way to the cottage, hoping that whoever lived inside might be able to tell her hexactly which story she was in. Even though the front door was open, she knocked on it and called inside, "Is anyone home?" Rosabella was fairy polite.

But no one answered.

She knocked again. She peeked through the open door into the cozy cottage. No one seemed to be there. She hesitated. The fireplace was roaring and the table was set. Whoever lived here had left in a hurry, and they might need Rosabella's help when they got back.

Something strange was happening in this forest. Maybe she could find a clue inside that would tell her where she was…and why the animals in this mysterious forest were all so scared!

CHAPTER 3

On the Case

Oh my wand! thought Rosabella as she walked into the cottage. Everything in it was enormous. An umbrella twice as tall as she was leaned against the wall. The furniture towered over her. A fire roared in a giant fireplace. Three big chairs were arranged around it. The biggest was so gigantic that Rosabella could have curled up on it with a bunch of her friends!

"Maybe giants live here!"

But she hadn't seen any beanstalks when she was walking through the woods—and the house didn't smell like giants. It smelled… cozy. She inhaled the sweet aroma that had lured her into the cottage and followed the smell to a bright kitchen.

There was a jar of honey on the table so huge, it could have fed every student at Ever After High. On the stove, a bubbling pot was sending up puffs of delicious steam. Rosabella pushed an oversize stool to the stove and stood on it to look inside. Was it an enchanted potion? Did a witch live here, perhaps?

Rosabella peeked inside the pot. Porridge! She sniffed. Porridge with honey! That's what smelled so sweet. Her tummy rumbled again.

She studied the kitchen table. There were three chairs—big, bigger, and biggest. There were three bowls on the table—big, bigger, and biggest. Steam wafted up from them. Someone had served the porridge into each of the bowls.

"Hello!" Rosabella called out. But no one was home. How strange! Who would leave the door open, a fire burning, and their hot breakfast on the table? As soon as she caught the scent of one mystery, another one popped up! Whom did the house belong to? And even more important, where were they?

Standing on the chair in front of the biggest bowl, she touched the side to test the temperature. Way too hot! Then she felt the medium-size bowl and found that it was way too cold. Finally, she felt the smallest bowl. It was just the right temperature! Rosabella dipped a spoon into the bowl to take the teeniest, tiniest taste. *Porridge with honey, just as I suspected,* she thought.

"Porridge that's just the right temperature," Rosabella said to herself. *"Just right."* Wait a minute! She knew this story. She looked around the room again. How had she missed it? Three chairs, three bowls of porridge. A giant jar of honey. There was even a painting on the wall of a friendly family of bears. Momma Bear was wearing an apron and had her arm around Baby Bear. Poppa Bear had a big smile on his face and was wearing a pointy green hat. The family looked so nice.

This must be Blondie Lockes's story: Goldilocks and the Three Bears!

Rosabella thought for a moment. The instructions for the midterm hexam were to get to The End of the storybook, but Rosabella couldn't fairy well worry about that after seeing the whole forest in such a tizzy! That sounded off-story, even for Goldilocks and the Three Bears. Where had the Bears gone, and whatever-after was going on? Rosabella was worried that the Bears had left their delicious breakfast without eating. They must have left in a hurry. Could this have something to do with why all the animals in the forest were so upset?

Rosabella decided that her first job was to figure out what happening and help any

animals that needed her. Then she could figure out how to pass her hexam and return to
Ever After High!

Rosabella searched the room carefully for a
clue, but she couldn't find anything that hexplained why the Bears had left. Besides, her
stomach was still rumbling, and it was hard to
think on an empty stomach. Tired, Rosabella
took a seat in Baby Bear's armchair (Poppa's
chair was much too hard, and Momma's was
too soft) and rested for a moment. It felt just
right.

Her thoughts turned to the porridge. It
had been delicious, but Rosabella would've
added some cream and maybe a touch of
cinnamon. That would have made it hextra
yummy. She rested her head on her hand and

thought about warm porridge in her stomach. She was beginning to feel a little bit sleepy. What a long, strange morning it had been. She was completely hexhausted.

It couldn't hurt to take a little nap....

And with that, she fell fast asleep. Her glasses slipped off her nose and landed on the floor.

CHAPTER 4

The Plot (and the Porridge) Thickens

Rosabella was dreaming she was in her own forest again. She walked past the big, old fir trees, past the rose garden, up to the castle with the huge front door. She pushed on the door, but it wouldn't budge. She reached up to the knocker above her head.

Knock, knock, knock, KNOCK!

Knock, knock, knock, KNOCK!

The noise woke up Rosabella. It wasn't

coming from her dream. It was coming from somewhere inside the house. Jumping out of the chair, she heard the front door slam shut.

Something fairy fishy is definitely up, thought Rosabella. *Was that the Bear family? Why didn't they say hello? Maybe because they couldn't see me.... But why did they leave so quickly?*

Rosabella raced to the window and peered through the glass. But—uh-oh!—she'd lost her glasses again. Everything was so foggy. She could hear leaves rustling, but she couldn't see anything hexcept trees and a shadow moving through the forest.

How was she going to solve a mystery if she couldn't see any clues? She found her way back to the chair where she'd been sleeping. They must have fallen off. She felt around on the floor...and discovered her glasses broken into two pieces! Rosabella didn't remember stepping on them. She held the pieces in front of her eyes and looked around the room.

All the chairs were toppled over. Feathers from burst pillows floated through the air. What had happened? Someone—or some*thing*—had stomped through the cottage in a hurry. Maybe that was what had happened to her glasses.

The living room looked like it had been hexed. It was a complete mess! The kitchen, too, was topsy-turvy—all the porridge in the bowls and in the pot was gone. Someone had used the tablecloth as a napkin and spilled the jar of honey all over the floor and knocked the Bear family portrait off the wall. How could someone have made such a big mess when she'd only closed her eyes for a moment?

Then Rosabella remembered the animals chattering about their damaged nests and dens. Whoever was causing so much trouble in the forest must've made the mess in the cottage! But why would someone want to do that?

Oh, this poor family, thought Rosabella. *I wouldn't want to come home to this mess and no breakfast!*

Well, what are Ever After High students good at? Solving problems! Suddenly, her frown flipped upside down. All the cottage needed was a little elbow grease, and it would be tidy in no time.

With a spoon, she scraped some hextra-sticky honey out of the jar and used it to glue her glasses back together. "I guess this trick will have to do!" she said out loud.

Smiling, she looked in the kitchen closet and found some cleaning supplies. *I can make sure they come back to a cleaner house and a better meal than they left behind in the first place! They sure look like a nice family. I hope we all can be friends.*

She washed the bowls and rinsed the tablecloth. She brought it outside to dry. In the front yard she spotted some pretty daisies, which she picked and put in a vase on the kitchen table. Everything looked in order!

"Now for the porridge!" Rosabella declared. She couldn't wait to get some porridge on the stove, and to eat some once the Bears were back home! She tried on Momma Bear's apron, but it was as big as a tent. She wrapped it around and around her dress.

Soon the kitchen smelled spicy and sweet. The porridge bubbled.

Rosabella stuck her finger in the big pot and took a taste. "A little too bland!" She put some more honey in and stirred. "That's better!" She added a dash of this, a little of that, a bit of charm, and some hextra-special love. It was going to be wonderful!

Now it was time to put the living room back in order. She was picking up a bear-size broom when she heard the front door squeak open.

"Who's there?" growled a grumbly voice.

Rosabella shivered.

She held on tight to the broom. She took a deep breath and tiptoed out of the kitchen and down the hallway.

Who was there? Was it the Bears? Or had the intruder returned?

Maybe this was the answer to the mystery.

CHAPTER 5

The Bear Facts

Standing in the frame of the open door was the same Bear family Rosabella had seen in the painting. Hexcept they were a lot bigger—and they definitely weren't smiling.

The minute Rosabella walked into the room, Momma Bear squealed in terror. Baby Bear clutched his mother. Even Poppa Bear was trembling, although he stepped forward bravely, glowering. "Are you the one who's been causing so much chaos in our forest?" he demanded.

"Look at this living room! It's a complete disaster," wailed Momma Bear.

"Please don't blow down the rest of our house!" Baby Bear begged.

Rosabella could tell that, despite their frowns, these bears were fairy nice. She took a big breath.

"Don't be afraid," she said calmly. "You're right. Someone's made a terrible mess. But I was just cleaning it up. That's why I've got this broom. Come try the porridge I just made and you'll see. And speaking of seeing, look at my glasses." She pointed at her face, where the lopsided frames hung on her nose. "Whoever blew through this house like a tornado managed to break them, too!"

Poppa Bear's eyes narrowed suspiciously. Momma Bear bit her lip. Should they trust this tiny stranger? But Baby Bear was grinning. He could already smell the porridge... and it smelled especially delicious.

"And...and you're not that Goldilocks girl we've heard about? The one who causes all that trouble?" asked Momma Bear.

"Well, not really. It's kind of complicated, but I promise I didn't make *this* mess, and I won't be making *any* messes! I just want to help."

Hesitantly, the Three Bears came inside and followed Rosabella into the kitchen. Momma Bear pulled Baby Bear close, but her wary expression softened the moment she saw the daisies on the table. "How fableous! I love flowers. I can't believe I never thought of that."

Rosabella blushed. "Here, try this." She couldn't wait to share her fresh porridge with the Bear family.

Poppa Bear's nose twitched. "It smells... good," he said cautiously.

Carefully, Rosabella served each bear a bowl. She gave a piping-hot serving to Poppa Bear. "Wow! This is delicious," he enthused, "and it's as hot as I always like it!"

"Just right!" said Baby Bear, and he put his snout into the bowl to eat. Momma Bear tapped his head to remind him of his manners. Smiling sheepishly, Baby Bear picked up his spoon.

Rosabella handed the last bowl to Momma Bear. The porridge had cooled down enough for her to eat it the way she liked. Rosabella watched as Momma Bear carefully tasted a tiny bite. She pursed her lips. She swallowed. She smiled! "Such a careful chef would never have caused this disaster. And no one who makes such tasty porridge could be responsible for this disarray," she announced. "Whatever-after did you add to it?"

"Just a pinch of cinnamon, some of my other favorite spices, and a little bit of cream." Rosabella was happy to share her cooking tips.

Momma Bear continued to smile, but when she thought Rosabella wasn't looking, she added some more honey. Rosabella laughed to herself. Momma Bear must have a sweet tooth!

Poppa Bear had already finished his meal. He sat back in his chair and studied Rosabella.

"Well, if you were busy stirring up this porridge, then who was stirring up trouble? Who could've done this to our home?"

"I don't know," answered Rosabella. She was washing up the cooking pot in the sink. "But I heard some birds and squirrels talking about trouble in the forest when I arrived."

"We left the house in a hurry today because some of our friends' houses were blown down—nests in disarray, dens disturbed," Momma Bear hexplained sadly. "It's up to us Bears to keep everyone in the forest happy and safe."

"Maybe the creature that made the mess in our house *also* made a mess in the forest," noted Baby Bear, who had just finished his third helping of porridge.

"Now, *there's* a thought!" Poppa Bear thrust his paw into the air.

"I bet a real bad beast is responsible!" chimed in Baby Bear.

"*You're* a beast, Baby Bear," Momma Bear gently reminded him.

"Well, then!" Baby Bear said. "Someone *much* beastlier than me."

But Rosabella shook her head. "I'm sure there's some hexplanation. Within every beast there's always some beauty! It's not fair to assume that anyone is bad before we know all the facts. Maybe it's just a misunderstanding and there is no bad beast at The End of this story. But the only way we're ever-after going to find out is by getting to the bottom of this!"

The Bears all nodded and thumped the table with their big paws in agreement.

Rosabella beamed and dipped her spoon into her own bowl. Finally, after serving everyone else, she could take a bite.

"Wow!" She sighed. "Just right!"

CHAPTER 6

Just a Hunch

After the meal, Momma Bear and Poppa Bear stayed in the kitchen while Baby Bear and Rosabella sewed up the cushions on the armchairs.

"It's so rewarding when you can turn a wrong into a right," Rosabella said as she embroidered a little flower where the rip in a cushion had been.

"You're right," said Baby Bear, admiring Rosabella's work.

"But tell me more about what's going on in the forest. Who do you think is knocking down all the houses?" Rosabella asked.

"Let's see." Baby Bear rubbed his head as he thought. "I don't know about clues, but I certainly saw a lot of animals today. The rabbits kept hopping over my feet while I tried to ask them questions, and the chickadees wouldn't stop singing when I was asking for a bird's-eye view...but a bee did show me where I could find some fairy sticky honey."

Rosabella chuckled. "It sounds like you lost the plot! Did you make it back to your own story by The End?"

"I'm super sorry, Rosabella." He sighed. "So

much happened that it's hard to remember it all. After a long morning and a yummy breakfast, it all becomes a bit fuzzy...."

Just then, Rosabella's honey-repaired glasses fell apart and hit the floor with a clatter.

"Oh no! Speaking of fuzzy, this mystery is going to stay unsolved if I don't have my glasses." Rosabella knelt down to pick up the pieces.

"I think I can help!" Baby Bear held out his paws to Rosabella.

Rosabella handed him her broken glasses and watched carefully as he hexamined them.

"Believe me—every Bear knows how to fix little problems." Baby Bear held up the two pieces. "That's why we are in charge of keeping the forest happy and organized."

He reached into a drawer and pulled out a piece of gold wire. Wrapping it around the broken parts of the glasses, he quickly made them as good as new.

But within moments his happy smile had become a frown. "If only we could fix up the forest's blown-down houses just as easily as your glasses."

"Don't worry, Baby Bear. I'm sure we will soon solve this problem, too. We just have to stay focused." Rosabella put her glasses back on happily and blinked. "Now, is there anything else you can remember?"

Baby Bear scooted onto his comfortable chair. He put his paw up to his chin and scratched it. "There *was* something a little off-the-page that happened...." Baby Bear's eyes brightened. "A super-strange girl appeared out of nowhere! Everyone was talking about her, and nobody knows who she is! She fell through the trees and landed right next to a squirrel, and her glasses fell off...." Baby Bear covered his face with his paws. "That was you, wasn't it?"

Rosabella laughed. "It was, but you know what? You might just be on to something. I wonder..."

"Wonder what?" Baby Bear asked.

"I wonder if somebody *else* has stumbled into the wrong story. If *I* did, somebody else could have, too, right? And maybe that person wouldn't be as careful as I was to not make a mess."

"Maybe that's the answer to our mystery!" Baby Bear replied.

"Baby Bear, I think it's time to rally the troops." Rosabella dusted off her dress. "We have to begin our investigation!"

And they bounded off to the kitchen to tell Poppa Bear and Momma Bear about their new lead!

CHAPTER 7

Ever After Evidence

A delicious smell greeted Rosabella and Baby Bear as they entered the kitchen.

"I think Momma Bear made some more porridge!" Baby Bear said hexcitedly. He rubbed his stomach, ready to eat another meal.

"I'm glad," Rosabella said, though she was still fairy full from breakfast. "We'll all need to keep up our energy if we're going back into the forest to search for another mysterious character on the loose."

Baby Bear was even happier to see that Momma Bear had prepared a little spell-ebration in honor of cleaning up the house. There were china cups filled with steaming tea and some cakes alongside more porridge! The porridge smelled hexceptionally good to Rosabella. This was just what they needed before starting their investigation.

The Three Bears enjoyed the porridge while Rosabella drank some warm tea. She smiled and thought, *These bears are always hungry! I guess if I were responsible for such a big forest, I'd have a big appetite to match!*

"Momma Bear, what secret ingredients did

you add to this batch?" Rosabella asked as she breathed in the delicious smell.

Momma Bear was wearing her flowery apron, which was just the right size on her. She grinned. "I took your advice about the cinnamon and the cream, but I also added some berries and maple syrup!"

Rosabella made a mental note of Momma Bear's recipe and thought, *Maybe I can make some porridge for my classmates in Princessology when I get back to Ever After High. This may not be my original tale, but you can always learn something new from new friends.*

As they finished up their meal, Baby Bear hexplained to his parents Rosabella's idea to go to the forest and investigate further. Poppa Bear patted Baby Bear's shoulder and nodded. He thought that sounded like a great plan!

In the forest, the trees waved their colorful leaves and the flowers swayed in the wind. Momma Bear picked a few flowers and tucked them into her cap for decoration.

Rosabella noticed bushes knocked over sideways and birds' nests on the ground. Everything was jumbled!

"Look!" cried Baby Bear. "The rabbits' den has been stomped on. They aren't even home. The rabbit family must have been afraid and run away!"

Momma Bear put her paw over her mouth in surprise, and Poppa Bear shook his head.

"This is totally unjust!" Rosabella was really upset now. She was fairy passionate about critters' rights, and it wasn't right (or, as Baby Bear would say, *just right*) that all these animals were having their homes, and lives, disturbed!

A family of foxes quietly emerged from the shadows of the trees. The one with the point-iest ears spoke up. "Our new house was just trampled! Will you help us, please?"

Rosabella knelt beside the fox and let him sniff her hand. "I promise I'll help you all. It's not fair that your homes are being destroyed, and we need to find whoever's doing this and give them a stern talking-to before the whole forest is destroyed."

The rest of the fox family cautiously came over to Rosabella. Poppa and Momma Bear gave them an approving nod, as if to say, *She's with us!* The littlest fox flicked his tail and jumped up on Rosabella's lap.

"Don't worry, foxes. We just need to get organized. The Three Bears and I are going to search the forest and see if anything else strange is going on."

"You mean like the strange girl?" squeaked the little fox. "The one the squirrels were talking about?"

Rosabella wondered if the squirrels had told the foxes about her landing in the forest earlier that day.

"That *could* be a lead. What did the girl look like?" Rosabella asked carefully.

"Everyone said she had long brown hair."

Rosabella looked at her own hair. Oh no. Maybe it wasn't a clue ever-after all.

"Did the girl have glasses?" asked Rosabella.

"Like yours? I don't think so. But she seemed kind of funny."

Whoever this mystery girl was, the only thing Rosabella knew for sure was that she'd have to talk to her. And to find the mystery girl, they had to talk to the squirrels right away!

The Three Bears led Rosabella down a path to a small woodland clearing filled with pink flowers. The squirrels were busy helping some cardinals put their nest back onto the branch of a tree.

"Oh no! Was your home blown down, too?" asked Poppa Bear, coming to the rescue. He helped put the nest on a higher branch. The squirrels squeaked in gratitude.

"*Cheep! Cheep!*" cried the cardinals as they hopped on and off Poppa Bear's shoulders. "We're *flight*fully grateful for your kind help, Mr. Bear!"

A squirrel looked over at Rosabella. "Hey! Princess! Did you find the right forest?"

Rosabella recognized the squirrel she had stumbled across right after she'd arrived in this topsy-turvy story! "Oh, hello again!" she answered, giving the squirrel a boost to a higher tree branch. "I don't think this is the *right* forest. But it's *just right* for right now. We're trying to solve the mystery of who's making a mess of everybody's homes."

"Ah!" Another squirrel pointed his bushy tail up in the air. "There's a nut that might help you with your next clue."

"Nuts!" hexclaimed Baby Bear, rubbing his stomach. He was always so fairy hungry. "That sounds delicious."

The squirrels all laughed, and the one who knew Rosabella called, "No! Not *that* kind of nut. There's a nutty girl who's helping critters rebuild their houses and painting them so beautifully that they're better than new! She knows so much about wood, you might think she was *made* of wood!"

Hmm...thought Rosabella. There was only one girl she knew who fit that description. And Rosabella had a feeling she wasn't the one stomping through the forest! "Can you help us find her?" she asked, and the squirrels all nodded in agreement

As they made their way through the trees,

Rosabella heard the sound of hammering…
and laughter.

A girl with long curly hair was helping
some rabbits rebuild the entrance to their
den. She was nailing the final touches to a
wooden archway. All around her were new
little birdhouses painted in a lovely array of
colors that matched the flowers nearby.

The girl clapped her hands hexcitedly
when she finished. "Why don't you guys hop
in and see how it feels?"

"Cedar!" hexclaimed Rosabella, recogniz-
ing her Ever After friend.

Cedar Wood did a double take. "Rosabella!
I'm so happy to see you!" Cedar ran to give
her friend a big, warm hug. Rosabella knew
Cedar really *was* glad to see her because

Cedar Wood, the daughter of Pinocchio, could never tell a lie.

"But wait a splinter! What are you doing here? I thought I was the only one going a little off book today."

Rosabella smiled. "We're more than just a little off-book. We're in a completely different book—Goldilocks and the Three Bears!"

"Wow! I wonder how we'll ever get back to Ever After High if we're not even in our own stories."

Rosabella had a few ideas about how to get to The End of this storybook and back to school, but she didn't want to leave until they could make this story a Happily Ever After for everyone!

"Rosabella, have you heard about what's

going on in the forest?" Cedar asked. "Houses are being knocked over and blown down! I don't remember that from Blondie's story. How can we turn it into a Happily Ever After when they've gone off script?"

Rosabella hexplained that something fairy strange was going on in this forest and she'd promised the Three Bears and all the woodland creatures that she would help put a stop to it. Maybe if they figured out what was going on, they could get the forest back on track!

Cedar was so happy that Rosabella wanted to help fix up the forest, too. "So many animals need their homes rebuilt. I was just starting to think I was the only girl around in this whole forest to help get the job done!"

"But we still don't know who is responsible for all this mess," Momma Bear said, sounding worried. She was picking up debris around the rabbits' den.

"Do you think a villain is on the loose?" Cedar asked with big, worried eyes.

"I just think there's a lot more to this story than we know right now. Have you seen anything unusual?" Rosabella asked Cedar.

Cedar tilted back her head thoughtfully. Her eyes brightened. "I did see *something*," she answered at last. "But I don't think any of the animals believed me when I told them about it."

Hearing this, the Three Bears turned to pay close attention to Cedar.

Cedar's face became serious. "It was scarier

than failing a hard hexam! Just after I spotted a bird's nest that had been knocked over, I saw a shadow of a big animal lumbering into the trees."

"Maybe there really *is* a villain in the woods!" Momma Bear bellowed.

Rosabella was worried. Cedar couldn't tell a lie, so now Rosabella knew for certain that there was a big animal knocking over houses. But she still didn't believe that anyone would intentionally cause so much trouble. No one would want to hurt such friendly creatures. Would they?

CHAPTER 8

The Scene of the Crime

"We can't have a villain in the forest!" Baby Bear said after thinking for a moment. "I've never met even one bad animal."

"Yes," Momma Bear added. "There are certainly countless animals in this forest, but none that are mean or hurtful."

"Deer, birds, skunks, foxes, rabbits, butterflies…" listed Poppa Bear, as though trying to see if he had forgotten any animals.

Baby Bear reached into the pocket of his shirt and then looked a bit embarrassed. "Can I show you guys something?"

"Sure thing!" Cedar and Rosabella said at the same time. Surprised, they shared a smile. They might not have been in the right story, but they were definitely on the same page.

Baby Bear took out a rolled-up piece of parchment that he stretched out slowly. A brightly colored map of the forest was painted on the parchment, with each critter and each critter's home carefully depicted.

"Oh my paws!" Momma Bear was surprised. "I've never seen *that* before, Baby Bear."

"I painted it," Baby Bear admitted bashfully. "I thought it might be helpful for finding our neighbors when they needed help."

"That's fairy considerate," Rosabella said

as she looked closer. There was even a small painted version of the Bears' cottage with a tiny painted Baby Bear standing outside the door.

Cedar hexamined the painting. "I don't see any villainous animals here, but I do see plenty of enchanting skill."

"You think so?" Baby Bear was skeptical. "I never thought I was any good at painting. I just like to play with colors. But I *bear*ly have enough brushes and paints to do another picture...."

"Trust me!" Cedar was really smiling now. "I love to paint, and this is impressive work. But don't worry. It would be my pleasure to help find you some more supplies."

"Really?" Baby Bear was brimming with delight.

"We'll be searching the forest to figure out who's knocking down houses. We can search for some art supplies for you, too, Baby Bear!" Rosabella decided on the spot.

All the animals cheered. One squirrel was so enthusiastic he fell off a branch and landed on Poppa Bear's head. Poppa Bear's green hat toppled to the ground, and he chuckled as the squirrel jumped down to retrieve it for him.

"Two stories are *almost always* better than one," Cedar said decisively. "Let's go!"

CHAPTER 9

The Unusual Suspects

Back at the cottage, Rosabella described a well-thought-out plan using Baby Bear's map. "All right, team! We have four hours until sunset, so there's a lot of ground to cover in fairy little time. Three Bears: You should go to the North Forest and the caves, since you know those places best. Cedar and I will go talk to the foxes, rabbits, and woodpeckers.

If anyone finds any leads, we can share them when we meet back here." Rosabella took a second to catch her breath. "Okay, break!" The Three Bears and the girls high-fived and went off into separate parts of the forest.

Rosabella and Cedar followed a long path along the side of a brook, on their way to check on some nearby fox dens. Rosabella was enjoying the sound of water rushing along the brook when suddenly they heard a big ruckus of squeaks.

"Stop stomping on our dens!"

"Leave our burrows alone!"

"You're the ones who are blowing down our homes!"

The rabbits were chittering at the foxes. The foxes were growling at the rabbits!

"You're sly foxes!" yipped a furious rabbit, thumping his hind legs angrily.

"It's you carrot-eaters who are ruining things!" sniffed a fox, glaring at them all.

Rosabella and Cedar had walked straight into a big argument between the rabbits and the foxes! Each group thought the other one was knocking over their homes, and neither would believe the other was innocent.

"Stop!" ordered Rosabella. This was just terrible! Everybody was blaming everybody else and nobody was listening. Houses could be repaired, but repairing friendships was often more challenging. "Now, listen here! I know that foxes and rabbits don't *always* get along, but everyone shares this forest, and it's just not right to blame one another without knowing the whole story. We're all worried about the forest, but we can make it better if we work together!"

The rabbits hung their heads, ashamed. The foxes frowned at their paws.

A rabbit with soft brown fur spoke up at last. "The foxes are always causing trouble for us. It must be them!"

"No fair!" A fox twitched his nose indignantly. "Just because we like to play doesn't mean we'd ever damage anybody's home! It's the rabbits who are always hopping without looking!"

"It wasn't us!" protested the littlest rabbit.

"Of course not," said Rosabella, giving the little rabbit a pat. "I don't think any of you would harm anybody else's home. I think, deep down, you all know that, too." She could see each animal's true character, and she knew that no one was at fault. But how could she persuade them to stop fighting?

"If we give everyone a chance to speak, maybe we'll learn something," she suggested.

"And remember: Honesty is always the best policy," Cedar told the animals cheerfully.

A rabbit cleared her throat. "We were playing all morning with the chipmunks, and when we got home, our dens were destroyed. Someone had stomped on them! The foxes must've—"

"Now, little rabbit. Stick to the facts," said Rosabella sternly.

But before the rabbit could continue, a family of crickets entered the glen. They were carrying small bags made of leaves over their shoulders.

"What's wrong?" Rosabella stepped carefully over to them.

"Some big animal just came and blew down our house," a cricket chirped. "We're moving to a new home!"

"How terrible!" all the animals cried out together.

"Wait a splinter..."

"What are you thinking, Cedar?" asked Rosabella. Everybody was quiet and gathered around to listen.

"Rewrite me if I'm wrong, but if somebody just blew down the crickets' house, then it can't be anyone who's here in this clearing," Cedar said.

"Whoops." A rabbit pulled at his ears. "I guess we were all hopping to conclusions."

Rosabella was feeling better now. "If we stop and listen to our forest creatures, we can solve this problem even faster."

"I guess I'm sorry," a fox said to a rabbit.

"We were royally wrong." A rabbit nodded while hopping up and down.

All the animals smiled, squeaked, and chattered with gratitude. Even though they hadn't found the mystery culprit yet, Cedar and Rosabella had still managed to help the forest. "Is there anything we can do to help you, too?" asked the rabbits and the foxes.

"There is one thing we need a little help with," said Cedar. "Our good friend Baby Bear is a wonderful artist, but he doesn't have enough painting supplies."

"I have some beaver friends who whittle paintbrushes with their teeth," a lady rabbit volunteered.

"The bumblebees know how to use pollen to make glittery paint," added a cricket.

"I know the woodpeckers love to collect birch bark that could be used as canvases," a fox suggested. "Let's help out our new friends and get Baby Bear some painting supplies!"

Rosabella and Cedar shared a grin. Everyone was getting along, and Baby Bear was one step closer to having enough painting supplies!

"Let's work together?" the littlest rabbit suggested to a fox.

"My paws, that's a great idea!" agreed the fox. Smiling and teaming up, the animals began to head off on their new quest.

Rosabella turned to Cedar. "I'm so glad none of our new friends were causing any trouble, but now we need to get back on the case. The crickets' home was just stomped on, and we still don't know who's making this mess!"

"I don't know what that shadowy thing was," Cedar responded. "But it still scares me."

Rosabella took a deep breath as they walked back into the forest.

Was someone going to jump out? Who was behind all this beastly behavior?

CHAPTER 10

Fowl Play

Next on their list were the woodpeckers. Cedar spotted some freshly pecked wood, and soon they were following the trail all the way into the deep forest. After a while, Cedar stopped and took a whiff of the fresh wood dust. "*Hmm*...I think they're close!"

Sure enough, just around a bend in the path, the woodpeckers were hammering away on a maple.

"Hello!" Rosabella called to them.

The woodpeckers paused. "Oh no! Oh no! Oh no!" they chattered nervously.

"Don't be frightened. We're not the ones knocking down houses," hexplained Rosabella.

Cedar nodded in agreement. "Actually, we're trying to find out who *is* responsible so we can stop them. We want to help fix up the forest!"

Reassured by the girls' friendly voices, the woodpeckers inched down the tree until they were eye level with the girls.

Some of the woodpeckers started chirping loudly. Others were nervously pecking away. "Our houses were just blown down from our trees!"

Rosabella was upset that the culprit had

struck again, but at last they were hot on the trail. They had their first clue! "Can you guys show us where your houses have been blown down?" she asked.

They followed the woodpeckers all the way to their trees, where a little house sat on the ground in a big mess. Cedar was sad to see a pretty house broken and covered in dirt on the ground.

Rosabella hexamined the destroyed pieces of the house for clues. She saw a big footprint, just like the big animal Cedar had seen. She looked at it more closely but couldn't tell what kind of animal had made it. It was too long for a bear, and too wide for a wolf. It didn't match any of the woodland creatures. They'd found a clue, but Rosabella had no idea what it could mean! All they really knew was that the animal Cedar had seen also knocked down these houses. And Rosabella still didn't know why.

"I'm so sorry this happened, my friends," Rosabella said gently.

The woodpeckers chirped in unison. "Do you know who could be huffing and puffing up all this trouble?"

"Oh, well, I *did* see a shadowy animal flee the scene of a crime earlier today," answered Cedar, honest as always.

The birds' feathers ruffled. They were upset again. This sounded scary.

"Deer me!" snorted a voice. A frightened deer standing on the tips of his hooves had arrived nearby. "That sounds like a big, bad wolf to me! That's what everyone is saying!"

"Did you say *a big, bad wolf?*" repeated Rosabella. "Has anybody seen one?"

The woodpeckers squawked and chattered. More deer appeared, stomping their hooves nervously. Everyone had an opinion, but nobody had a clue.

"Everyone should stay calm," Rosabella told the deer. "No one's seen a wolf, so we shouldn't assume a wolf is causing trouble. Besides, everybody makes mistakes sometimes. I'm sure the culprit didn't mean to damage anyone's home."

But still, Rosabella knew that whoever was knocking over houses needed to apologize to the whole forest. Everyone was fairy upset.

Noticing how upset the little birds were that their houses had been knocked down, Cedar wanted to help make them happy.

"Maybe I can fix these houses!" Cedar offered. "Can you help me find some paint, please?"

The woodpeckers all chirped happily, hexcited to have Cedar's help.

"Spelltacular!" Cedar clapped her hands. A red woodpecker flew off and returned quickly with some nutshells filled with an assortment of pretty colors.

Cedar got to work. Soon, with some help from the birds, she was hammering the house back together. With the paint she made sure the front door was a bright-blue and the roof was an enchanting mix of pinks and greens.

"Wow!" cried the red woodpecker and his friends when they saw Cedar's work. She was already weaving some broken nests back together. The woodpeckers all chirrupped and chirped their thanks. They saw that their homes were even prettier and sturdier now that Cedar Wood had reconstructed them.

"How can we repay you for all your help, Cedar?" the woodpeckers asked.

"Well, there's one thing you can do...." Cedar began. She had twigs and feathers in her hair after her hard work, but she seemed proud. She was really beginning to look like she belonged in this story!

"Tell us! Tell us!" the birds twittered.

"I may be good at painting, but Baby Bear is fairy talented, too! He paints the forest, including your homes and habitats, just like it really looks. But he needs more paints and brushes!"

"I swear by my feathers that we will find more painting supplies for Baby Bear than he'll be able to use," the red woodpecker promised.

"That's fableous!" Both Rosabella and Cedar smiled. They made a great team. Cedar could help return the forest to normal while Rosabella rallied everyone to solve the mystery. It was also fairy important that all the animals got along. Rosabella wanted to be sure no animal rights were taken away, even when things were so mixed up.

"I'm glad we're making a difference, but I still don't know whatever-after is at The End of this tale," Cedar wondered out loud as the woodpeckers headed off to find art supplies.

"I know," Rosabella agreed as she pushed her glasses farther up her nose. "I wish we could piece together this puzzle. But we won't give up until our work is done and the forest is secure again! Let's keep our eyes open and our mystery-solving skills sharp."

Rosabella and Cedar were more determined than ever-after!

CHAPTER 11

A Critter Culprit

Rosabella and Cedar continued on their search for answers in the forest. They walked along the brook, looking for clues. Rosabella was focused on a snapped twig in her path when suddenly she heard a loud rumbling from beside her. She jumped up, startled, before noticing that Cedar was rubbing her stomach.

"Sorry, Rosabella. I don't want to sound

discouraged, but I'm getting fairy tired and hungry," she admitted.

Rosabella was starting to get hungry, too. She hoped Momma Bear might have a fresh batch of porridge in the cottage. Just thinking about it was making her even hungrier. "Let's go back to the Bears' cottage and rest. Maybe the Bears had better luck finding clues than we did today."

"And maybe they'll have some snacks!" Cedar Wood said hopefully.

As they neared the warm and cozy Bear family home, the two girls caught a familiar smell. Momma Bear had some porridge on the stove!

"Hexcellent!" they both hexclaimed and then laughed.

"Is that our new friends I hear?" called Momma Bear from the front door. "I have some dinner ready to share."

"Let me guess," said Rosabella, chuckling. "Is it just right?"

"Just right you are!" Momma Bear answered. "I added some savory herbs from my garden and a pawful of walnuts."

Rosabella and Cedar helped Baby Bear set the table, and they all sat down for a yummy dinner. Everyone dug in, and after a second serving, Cedar held out her bowl for more. "It's just so good!"

"My paws!" Momma Bear beamed with pride. "I'm glad my recipe turned out so well."

Over their scrumptious dinner, the Three Bears caught the girls up on their progress.

They had talked to the other animals in the forest—the big moose and the twisty snakes, the wise owls and the playful otters. None knew who was causing the trouble. Momma Bear was beginning to suspect this mayhem wasn't being caused by *any* of the woodland creatures ever-after all.

Cedar chimed in. "We don't think any of the creatures are at fault, either. All the animals were just so nervous. But Rosabella helped everyone stay calm and friendly."

"Thanks, Cedar." Rosabella was blushing.

"It's true!" insisted Cedar. Everybody laughed, knowing she couldn't tell a lie.

After they finished eating, Momma Bear cleared the table, and then everyone helped out with the dishes. While Cedar and Rosabella finished cleaning up, Baby Bear sat in his chair and started painting. The foxes had already dropped off some canvases made of bark. Baby Bear nibbled the end of his brush, thinking hard about what to add to his picture.

He suddenly looked up from the canvas with bright eyes. "Cedar, would you mind helping me finish my painting? I'm not sure if there's something else I should add."

Cedar walked over to him and took in Baby Bear's artwork—and she was fairy surprised by what he had painted!

"Uh—Rosabella? I think you should take a look at this!" called Cedar.

Rosabella bounded over to look at Baby Bear's brand-new bark painting. It showed a familiar scene. Confused critters stood next to a pile of debris, another mess of blown-down houses. There was a shadowy wolf running off into the forest.

But those weren't just any old critters.

"Are those pigs?" asked Rosabella. "Are there three of them?"

Baby Bear nodded.

"But there aren't any piggies in our forest," Momma Bear noted.

"That's because this isn't a painting of *our* forest, Momma," said Baby Bear with a smile. "It's a painting of The Three Little Pigs. All these houses being blown down today reminded me of that fairytale!"

Rosabella took a closer look at the painting. After a moment, she finally realized that the colorful pile of debris the three pigs were

standing by was made up of straw, wood…
and bricks!

Rosabella started thinking out loud. "I'm
fairy certain I know what's going on in this
hextra mixed-up story!"

Cedar's eyes grew wide as she realized
what Rosabella was saying. "We're not just in
Goldilocks and the Three Bears—"

"We're in Goldilocks and the Three Little
Pigs!" announced Rosabella.

Their fairytale mix-up was mixed up with
another fairytale!

"Wait…" Poppa Bear furrowed his brow.
"I'm confused. What story is this?"

"It's two stories mixed up into one! In the
tale of The Three Little Pigs, a big, bad wolf
would huff and puff and blow all the houses

down!" hexplained Baby Bear as he pointed to his painting. "And in our tale, the forest houses keep getting blown down, too!"

"Oh. I see now," Poppa Bear said as he pulled at his chin whiskers. "So the Big Bad Wolf has been blowing down our forest homes?"

"I guess someone else ended up in the wrong story, too," considered Rosabella as she looked at the scary face of the wolf in Baby Bear's picture. "Still, I don't believe a big, *bad* wolf is responsible. Maybe a good wolf just got confused...."

"There's only one way to find out," replied Poppa Bear. "We've got to set a trap to catch him in the act. Then we can question him."

"If he's a smart wolf, we'll need a smarter plan to catch him," Momma Bear suggested.

As the Bear family and Cedar began to scheme, Rosabella stood aside and thought, *I just want to talk to the wolf! I'm sure if we listen, he can hexplain everything. I'm sure he's just as friendly as the other critters in this forest.*

CHAPTER 12

A Big, Bad Trap

Rosabella was filled with new energy and hexcitement after their tasty dinner and lucky break. They finally knew who was turning their pages!

"Everybody is getting better at understanding one another since you both showed up," noted Baby Bear. "The rabbits and the foxes are talking, and I even hear the woodpeckers are helping hammer together new birdhouses for the chickadees!"

"That's hexcellent! I couldn't wish for anything more." Rosabella was glad that the critters were beginning to realize that their forest neighbors were actually friendly and talented.

As they walked through the forest, more and more animals noticed them and began to ask questions. First a little hedgehog scuttled by their path, his quills standing up high.

"Don't worry, little hedgehog. We're just passing through to help!" said Rosabella before giving him a soft pat. The hedgehog gave a quiet squeak, happy that Rosabella had seen past his quills to his soft, fuzzy insides. With that, the hedgehog joined their group as they headed deeper into the forest to set their trap.

Noticing how friendly they were, the foxes and rabbits and deer and birds all began to follow. Finally, they came upon a group of bees and butterflies that were playing in the grass. Seeing Momma Bear—who always loved their honey—the bees flew over for a chat. The bees loved to share their honey with the Three Bears, and now they wanted to help find the wolf!

"Hey, little butterflies. Can you help us with something?" questioned Cedar as the butterflies gracefully floated by. She held out her colorful skirt, and the butterflies landed on it.

"Of course!" the butterflies agreed.

"We're trying to catch the shadowy animal that's been causing this forest so much trouble. We need to think of a trap to lure him out of the woods."

"A sticky trap! What about some honey?" one of the bees suggested.

Rosabella smiled at the idea. "I think the only critters we'd catch with honey would be a family of hungry bears."

"You are right about that!" Poppa Bear replied.

Baby Bear took out his painting of The Three Little Pigs and showed it to the bees and butterflies. "Somebody like the Big Bad Wolf is blowing down our houses. Maybe we can use this for inspiration."

The bees and butterflies hummed and bumbled close to the painting. They talked among themselves. Finally, they had an idea!

A butterfly perched on the edge of Cedar's skirt spoke up. "What does a big, bad wolf want more than anything?"

Poppa Bear looked stumped and rubbed his chin. "By my paws, I don't know."

Cedar's face lit up. "I know! He wants something to blow down!"

"Hexactly!" The butterfly beat her wings happily.

Rosabella thought for a moment. "We just need to make some houses that are so sturdy and pretty that the wolf won't be able to stop himself. He'll have to come and blow them down! Once we talk to him, we can finally figure this out." At last Rosabella saw how this story was coming together. "And we have all the skills to set this plan in motion. We can all gather the materials. Cedar can help us build the houses. And Baby Bear can use his new paint to make them colorful and inviting!"

Poppa Bear patted his pointy green hat and hexclaimed, "Well, let's get started!"

Everybody got to work turning the woodsy clearing into three houses.

"Let's be fairy hexact and make the houses just like the ones in the story," suggested Rosabella. Baby Bear nodded as he started mixing up some paints the birds had just delivered.

"One straw house, one wood house, and one brick house?" asked Cedar as she started to build the foundation of a house with Momma Bear's help.

"You've got it," said Rosabella.

In no time, three houses with red, green, and blue roofs stood in the clearing.

"Flying five," cried a woodpecker, raising his wing and trying to high-five Cedar.

Cedar gently tapped his wing and laughed. "We all make a really good team. It's a shame these houses have to be blown down."

"We can always fix them back up!" suggested the hedgehog from the ground. He had just finished weaving a wreath to put on the last house's front door. The entire forest had never had so much fun working together.

"Quick!" called Rosabella. She gathered her friends. "Let's hide in the bushes until our culprit shows up."

In a hurry, they all scattered to find a hiding spot behind a tree, flower, or bush. The

Bears apparently thought a patch of sunflowers were enough to keep them hidden. With a smile, Rosabella hexplained, "You guys need to shrink or find some bigger flowers to hide behind."

Bashfully, the Three Bears moved to hide in the shadow of a couple large oak trees.

"I'm nervous, Rosabella," whispered Baby Bear. "What if the Big Bad Wolf really *is* big and bad?"

"Don't worry, Baby Bear. We have the whole forest with us. And besides, I'm fairy certain nobody bad is responsible for this mess. Let's stay quiet so we don't scare *him* off."

Finally, everybody was quiet, and the houses sparkled with their new paint.

They waited, and they waited…and they

waited. They were getting sleepy, and some of them, mainly Baby Bear, were getting a little grumpy from hunger. The sun was sinking lower and lower.

Rosabella let out a disappointed sigh. Maybe this plan wasn't tricky enough.

All of a sudden, a loud *crack* and *whoosh* sounded from the other side of the clearing.

The birds chirped in surprise.

Huff, puff, huffing puffing. Someone was out of breath.

Oh no! thought Rosabella. She was a little bit scared.

Maybe it really was a big, bad wolf!

CHAPTER 13

Cold Case

Every critter was trembling. Rosabella waved silently at the birds, and they stopped chirping.

Who was huffing and puffing up to the houses?

Rosabella reached out for Cedar's hand. Cedar squeezed Rosabella's hand back. *It's good to have a friend here with me,* thought Rosabella.

All of a sudden, there was a huge gust of wind and straw.

KERCHOOOOO!

When the dust settled, everybody jumped out in order to catch the wolf in the act. They were finally going to learn who was causing all this trouble, and figure out why!

"Freeze! Hands up!" called out Poppa Bear.

Baby Bear, who had jumped out from the trees too quickly, fell over. He rolled into a somersault and stood up, looking dizzy.

"Wait a splinter..." Cedar gasped. "That's not a big, bad wolf."

"It's not a big, bad wolf ever-after all!" cried Rosabella with happiness. She'd known in her heart that no one bad could be causing this trouble!

"Where…am…I?—*KERCHOO!*" sneezed the shadowy animal. Hexcept it wasn't a shadowy animal. It was Daring Charming, transformed again into Daring the Beast! He'd sneezed his way through the forest and knocked down yet another house!

Rosabella blushed. After all, Daring just might be her prince. But looking at him now, it seemed he still had a little Beast left in him. Not to mention, quite the cold!

"Daring?"

But Daring Charming was fairy confused. He looked around the clearing with his red, runny eyes.

Cautiously, Rosabella stepped into the clearing and Daring caught sight of her for the first time.

"Rosabella!" hexclaimed Daring as he wiped his beastly nose on his sleeve. "I've been searching for our castle *all day long*. It's positively hexhausting. It's bad enough that I'm a Beast again, but now I have a *cold*! Everything is terrible."

"But, Daring…this isn't Beauty and the Beast! We're in Goldilocks and the Three Little Pigs…well, kind of, anyway. And you've been huffing and puffing and blowing these houses down all day with your big sneezes."

He scratched his head with his big paw and frowned. His nose dripped. "I thought I was in my own forest the whole time. I didn't think anyone would mind if *the Beast* let out a few sneezes. But now I guess I sneezed so hard I ended up in the wrong story!"

"You're in *our* forest," rumbled Momma Bear as all the woodland critters gathered around her. "And you've made quite the mess!"

Daring looked around thoughtfully, noticing the pile of straw and the upset rabbits and foxes and birds. "Did I really make this whole mess?"

Cedar chimed in to answer honestly. "Yes, you did," she said sadly. "Your beastly sneezes caused a big, bad disaster. It looks like you've been more of a Beast than a prince lately."

If there was one thing Daring wanted to be good at, it was acting like a prince. He looked so upset that the Bears began to soften and smile.

"It's okay," piped up Baby Bear at last. "We all make mistakes sometimes."

"Here you go," added a rabbit. He produced a handkerchief made of leaves and flowers. "You can wipe your nose on this." Daring's cold was dreadfully un-charming.

KERCHOO! Daring let out another loud sneeze that shook the leaves right off a tree.

"My paws!" said Momma Bear. She rested a paw on Daring's big, furry shoulder. "It sounds like you have a terrible cold. We can take care of you at the cottage."

"Why, tha-tha-thank you—*KERCHOO!*" And with one big sneeze, Daring blew over the wooden house and the brick house, right down to the grass.

Glancing around at the frustrated animals and noticing Rosabella's disapproving look, Daring laughed awkwardly. "Well, haha, I guess I need to learn to cover my nose!"

CHAPTER 14

The Beast Bust

Once everyone realized that Daring the Beast wasn't trying to cause trouble, the animals calmed down and started to clean up the mess. The bees and butterflies were busy trying to reconstruct the straw house's front porch, while the deer and beavers did some heavy lifting with the wood and bricks. After all, these would be fairy nice houses for someone!

Daring was sitting on a log all alone, embarrassed by his dripping nose and destructive sneezes. Rosabella sat down beside Daring and caringly put an arm around his shoulders. "Daring, it's true you may have been in the wrong story. But you still caused a lot of trouble. It's important to treat every forest and fairytale with respect. Especially if it's not your own."

Daring blinked at her. Then he slowly nodded. "Yeah. You're right, Rosabella. I might not have been fairy charming today...*ker-ker...kerchoo!*" This time he covered his nose.

"If you're going to be a ruler one day, you have to start thinking about others—even when you're feeling a little off book."

She reached into the pocket of her dress

and pulled out some cough drops. Rosabella was always prepared to help someone in need. "Here, take some of these. They'll make you feel better."

He popped a cough drop in his mouth. "Yum! Great!"

"Uh, I think you're forgetting something, Daring," Cedar said, overhearing their conversation.

"Oh…yeah. Thank you, Rosabella!"

"You're welcome." Rosabella appreciated Daring's gratitude. "But isn't there something you're forgetting to say to everyone else?" Rosabella hoped Daring had learned something about being considerate of others.

But Daring wasn't getting the picture. Sucking on the cough drops and blowing his nose, he looked at everyone. Then he caught a glimpse of his dirty clothing. He definitely didn't look like a dashing prince! He scratched his head. "Hey, guys. It would be spelltacular if you could find me some more princely clothes and a down-feather bed and a cup of hot chocolate. Obviously, it's been a hexing day for me." Then he lay back on the log and bit down on his cough drop.

The Bear family blinked at him. Cedar's mouth hung open in surprise.

He tried to flash his dazzling smile, but his drippy nose made him look pretty silly.

"And while we're at it"—he looked directly at Rosabella—"some more of these delicious cough drops would help."

Everyone just stared at Daring. The crickets started chirping.

"What am I doing wrong?" he asked. He rubbed his red nose before sneezing again. The birds all flew in front of the wooden house, protecting it from Daring's huffs and puffs.

"Daring, I think you're forgetting that you're not the prince in this story. And while all that huffing and puffing was no fun for you, it was even *less* fun for the creatures in this story. Remember, you knocked down a bunch of houses, and you made a big, bad mess of things. Maybe you should say something to everyone who lives in this fairytale."

Daring wrinkled his brow. His mouth dropped open, revealing his bright-white teeth. "Oh…I see! Wow. What a disaster I've caused. I knew I sneezed up a storm, but I hadn't really thought about how that would affect everyone else…"

Rosabella's eyes lit up! Daring was finally getting it. She gave him an encouraging smile.

"…and I should…*apologize*! That's it! Critters and creatures! I am really sorry for the mayhem and mischief I caused. I didn't realize what I was doing, but that doesn't make it okay. I want to be a good prince and a good Beast one day." Daring caught Rosabella's eye and she blushed. "And that means caring about everyone."

"Hexactly!" the Bear family seconded. "And as the forest guardians, we accept your apology."

"I'll try to help clean up the chaos, and I'll

be hexceptionally careful not to disturb any-one else's story in the future."

The animals welcomed his apology and started to bark, tweet, and cheer. Cedar clapped her hands in delight. "Fableous!"

Rosabella took Daring's hand and squeezed it. "That was a great apology, Daring. And what you just said was fairy princely to me. Just think about how impressed all the other princes will be when you get back to Ever After High."

Obviously, the idea of royally impressing his classmates cheered up Daring. He grinned. "You're right! And I'm thankful that you stopped me before I toppled any more houses." He covered his mouth and let out another big sneeze, then wiped his running nose on his sleeve. "But feeling good in my heart is not making my cold go away any faster. This cold is royally terrible!" A bird came to sit on his shoulder.

"You poor prince!" Momma Bear hexclaimed with her paws in the air. "Let's get you back to our cottage. I'll cook up some vegetable soup for your cold."

"And a side of porridge, pretty please!" requested Poppa Bear. "I'm getting hungry after all this commotion."

"That sounds just right," Daring responded, and everybody started to head back through the trees to the Bear family home.

"Hey, Daring?" asked Cedar. "Don't you have a royally amazing collection of paintings in your castle?"

"Yeah! I do. Lots of handsome portraits of me sitting and standing and lying down, wearing my gold crown and my silver crown. Oh, and one with my special diamond-encrusted crown! And there are a few other paintings and stuff," hexplained Daring.

"Wow," said Baby Bear. He was clutching some new paintbrushes the beavers had made for him.

"Baby Bear loves to paint. He might learn a lot by studying those, uh, works of art..." suggested Cedar.

"Of course! That's a great idea," agreed Daring, and he immediately started talking to Baby Bear about his painting hobby.

"Maybe you can paint me into your pic-ture," Daring proposed, taking a long look at

Baby Bear's forest scene. "But you'll have to make me hextra handsome…and maybe a little less hairy."

Everybody laughed. Daring Charming had apologized, but he was still himself. Even when he had a runny nose!

CHAPTER 15

Story Solved

As they made their way back to the cottage, Momma Bear and Poppa Bear kept inviting more and more critters to dinner.

"It's the right time for a spellebration!" said Poppa Bear after he had spread the word to a family of deer.

Cedar was so happy that the search for Baby Bear's painting supplies had worked.

The forest critters came to the spellebration with bags full of new supplies for him to use. The otters from the brook were especially hexcited to help out Baby Bear.

"We took some of the reeds from the shore and made fine-tipped brushes for small details," an otter said.

Soon every critter had arrived. They had canvases made of bark and leaves for Baby Bear, and the butterflies brought the most beautiful assortment of paints made from flower pollen.

Baby Bear kept blushing. "I'm so grateful for you guys. Who knows how I would have kept painting without your help?"

"I'm sure you would have figured out a way," responded Cedar. "But having friends makes everything better. I wonder how long it would have taken to solve this mystery if the whole forest hadn't worked together to figure it out."

"I would have blown down so many more houses!" hexclaimed Daring. He wiped his nose on a handkerchief and glanced at Rosabella to see if she was impressed.

"Let's not worry about what could have happened, and spellebrate what *did* happen! Thanks to some unhexpected characters, it looks like this story will have a happy ending ever-after all," Momma Bear said from beside the stove. She was chopping up vegetables for Daring's soup, and Daring had even volunteered to help.

"As long as you promise not to sneeze into

this soup," Momma Bear had warned. Daring wore Poppa Bear's apron while he cooked.

"You actually look a little dashing in that apron," joked Rosabella. But it was true. She liked Daring better when he was lending a helping hand, even as a Beast.

"Really? Do I dazzle? How's my fur?" he immediately asked. "Do you have a mirror?"

Rosabella just rolled her eyes and laughed.

Meanwhile, Baby Bear and Cedar were busy in the living room, setting up an easel the beavers had made. "I'm going to paint a picture for everybody who helped me out," decided Baby Bear.

When the food was ready, Baby Bear didn't even notice. He was too busy painting a picture of their new story's ending. It was a painting of everybody spellebrating in the Bear family kitchen.

Rosabella peeked her head into the living room and saw the painting. "That's just right, Baby Bear. You're really talented. You even remembered to add the red highlights in my hair!"

"This is all thanks to you! You were really great at helping everyone be more understanding of one another. If it weren't for you, the whole forest might not be spellebrating tonight!" responded Baby Bear, brushing some paint from his paws.

"That's a fairy sweet thing to say, Baby Bear. I think the forest is in great hands with you." Rosabella gave him a warm hug. "It's time to eat, though. Can you take a break?" she asked.

"Definitely. I'm always ready for some more porridge." He stood up quickly and almost knocked over his easel.

In the kitchen, it was just like Baby Bear's painting. The birds were flying around with the salt and pepper shakers. Poppa Bear was serving everybody bowls of porridge. Daring seemed much better as he sipped on his soup. His nose was returning to a regular color.

Rosabella sat down next to Cedar. "Cedar, you've been an enchanting mystery-solving partner."

"You too, Rosabella! I'm glad this mix-up happened so we had the chance to find out what a good team we make."

"Definitely," said Rosabella, yawning. After a bite of porridge, she was beginning to feel fairy sleepy. It had been a long day with a lot of plot twists. "But we still haven't figured out how to complete our midterm hexam and get back to Ever After High." As Rosabella spoke, her eyes were fluttering closed.

"Rosabella! It looks like you might fall asleep face-first into your porridge bowl!" hexclaimed Momma Bear.

Rosabella quickly startled awake. But almost instantly, her eyes began closing again.

Baby Bear giggled softly. "It looks like Rosabella Beauty is becoming Sleeping Beauty," he joked.

"Rosabella, how about you go upstairs and take a nap in a bed?" suggested Momma Bear. "We can worry about getting you home tomorrow."

"S...s...sounds good," sighed Rosabella,

and she waved good-bye to all her new friends before heading upstairs.

The Bear family beds were just like the Bear family! There was a huge bed for Poppa Bear, a big bed for Momma Bear, and a smaller bed for Baby Bear. She slid into Baby Bear's bed. It was super soft and comfortable.

"Wow!" declared Rosabella. "This bed is just right for me."

In a few seconds, she was fast asleep.

WHOOOOOSH!!!

The moment Rosabella fell asleep, she found herself back in her Ever After High classroom. She must have made it to The End!

Cupid ran over to Rosabella's side.

"Rosabella! Were you in a fairytale mix-up,

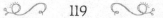

too? What happened? How did you get to The End?" Cupid asked all at once.

"Wait a spell…" Rosabella said, looking around. "That was a surprising end to the story!"

But then Rosabella spotted Daring and Cedar sitting behind her, looking just as confused. Daring still had a spoon full of soup in his hand. Rosabella realized that she'd finished the fairytale in her own special way! She'd tried the porridge, she'd sat in a cozy chair, and finally, she'd slept in a Bear family bed. But that wasn't the whole picture. In fact, Goldilocks and the Three Little Pigs ended up being more of an adventure than Rosabella could've ever imagined. She'd helped Baby Bear continue painting, solved a mystery with Cedar's help, and even made Daring a more thoughtful prince! *That's a fairy happy ending ever-after all,* she thought.

"You know, Cupid?" Rosabella said. "Sometimes the wrong fairytale turns out to be just right!"